Fastback Beach

Shirlee Smith Matheson

orca soundings

ORCA BOOK PUBLISHERS

Copyright © 2003 Shirlee Smith Matheson

National Library of Canada Cataloguing in Publication Data
Matheson, Shirlee Smith

Fastback Beach / Shirlee Smith Matheson.

(Orca soundings)

1-55143-267-6

I. Title. II. Series.

PS8576.A823F37 2003   jC813'.54   C2003-910688-8

PZ7.M42477Fa 2003

First published in the United States, 2003

Library of Congress Control Number: 2003105878

Summary: When Miles is put on probation for stealing a car, he learns about hot rods and rebuilding cars. When the project is stolen, Miles has to face up to his friends.

Orca Book Publishers gratefully acknowledges the support for its publishing programs provided by the following agencies: the Government of Canada through the Book Publishing Industry Development Program (BPIDP), the Canada Council for the Arts, and the British Columbia Arts Council.

Cover design: Christine Toller
Cover photography: Eyewire
Printed and bound in Canada

05 04 03 • 5 4 3 2 1

IN CANADA:
Orca Book Publishers
1030 North Park Street
Victoria, BC Canada
V8T 1C6

IN THE UNITED STATES:
Orca Book Publishers
PO Box 468
Custer, WA USA
98240-0468

PAPERBACK

To Billy and Brooklyn

Chapter One

The Mustang convertible sits in the parking lot of the ten-story apartment building, nicely hidden from view by a huge leafy poplar tree.

"Like it, Miles?" asks Larry the Lark.

"Sweet," I say.

Black paint gleams in the moonlight, shiny and sleek. I look up at the apartment block. Blinds are closed on most windows. The others are in darkness. No one is sitting out on balconies. It's 11:00 at night. All good people are in their beds.

Spider throws down his smoke and grinds the butt with his heel. "Let's move."

There's no backing down. Larry is already checking the doors. "Locked," he mutters.

"No problem." Spider pulls a tool from a duffel bag he's carrying.

"He's got a Slim-Jim," Larry whispers for my education.

"Forget that!" Spider says. "It's a *ragtop*, man!"

He is holding something in his hand. I hear a click and a long thin blade flashes out. Spider leans over the roof and I hear the rip as he slashes the tight canvas top. He reaches in to pull up the lock and in a split second he's yanking the door open.

Larry spins around the front of the car and jumps into the passenger side.

"It's Clubbed!"

"No sweat. Good scouts come prepared," says Spider. He grins — the first time

I have seen a smile crack his face. He yanks up his sleeve and rips off a hacksaw blade that is taped to his forearm. He starts sawing at the wheel. There must be only a thin circle of metal under the padding. After just a minute of intense work, Larry spreads the wheel apart and Spider removes the Club. They work like a team. They must have done this before.

What am I doing here? I stand in the shadow of the tree. My mind is racing. My heart is pounding. It's happening. And I'm in.

Larry reaches over to the steering column with a screwdriver and breaks the ignition lock. Spider flings the Club into the backseat and slips the five-speed gearshift into neutral.

"Push!" Spider hisses. I go around to the back. Together we roll the car out of the parking lot and into the darkened alley. "Get in!"

I scramble into the backseat. Spider and Larry jump in the front. Before the doors are closed, Larry sticks the screwdriver into the ig-

3

nition switch, the engine roars to life and we're spewing gravel.

When we're a couple of blocks away, Spider screeches to a stop. "Let's get some moonshine." I think he means booze, but his plan is to lower the top. Moonlight suddenly washes over us in a silver glow.

"Beauty!" Spider says as we hit the freeway. "No more second-rate junkers for us!"

I sit forward and watch the speedometer climb. Then Spider floors it. I fall back onto the leather seat.

"Hey, slow down!" I shout.

"You *like* speed!" Larry yells back. "Your old man's a racer."

"Yeah, but on a racetrack. This . . ." Another acceleration throws me back again.

How did I get into this? How do I get out? *Will* I get out? Spider is screaming and yelling like some freak, which he is. Larry has been my friend since first grade, even though he's gone a bit crazy since his parents split up. His mother moved off and took his little sister. He lives with his dad who lets him run wild.

"Go, man!" Larry yells and taps a drum-beat on the dashboard with his fingers. It drives me crazy when he does that, as if he's some kind of rock band drummer.

At the turnoff to Fastback Beach, Spider stomps the brakes and the car fishtails. He straightens it but we've passed the turnoff, so he cuts a U-turn in the middle of the highway, laying rubber that smokes around us. Then we're on the gravel trail leading down to the beach.

Below us, white in the moonlight, stretch miles of sand. This is a perfect place for drag racing. Spider steps on it and the car jumps ahead. I put my hand down for balance and it touches something soft on the seat. I hold it up. A kid's teddy bear. Aw, jeez, we've stolen some family guy's car. I throw the bear onto the floor and brace as we hit a dune and become airborne.

Spider yells and laughs as he spins another donut. Sand fills the air. "Hey, bro, your turn!" He and Larry fling open the doors and do a fast runaround to exchange seats. Larry floors it and misses the shift into second. The engine screams and the car lurches like it might fold double.

I yell, "Stop!" Larry does. I'm thrown between the two front bucket seats, my head connects with the upper edge of the windshield and I'm out cold.

A light shines in my face. My eyes water and my head pounds.

"Kid's hurt. Call an ambulance," a deep voice growls. I hear someone talking on a radio. I try to sit up. Can't.

I'm sprawled across the front bucket seats of the Mustang with my legs hanging out the open driver's door. I throw my hand over my eyes to shut out the light.

"Well, kid, you got some 'splainin' to do!" Someone's being funny, sounding like Desi talking to Lucy on those old reruns Mom watches. I try to sit up. My head, half-stuck under an armrest, threatens to explode so I lie back again. I hear sirens but I can't move.

The passenger door is thrown open and my head falls back. A guy stares down at me.

"Careful here! Head injury. Could be vertebrae damage. *Stretcher!*" He snaps the command and my lights blink out.

Chapter Two

"Miles John Derkach, you are charged with theft over $5,000. How do you plead?"

"Guilty."

Mom gasps from behind me. She wanted to hire a lawyer but I said no. The lawyer would discover I wasn't alone, maybe that I wasn't even driving.

I glance back to see Mackenzie sitting beside Mom. She gives me a small encouraging smile. "Kenny" and I have been dating for four months. Great way to impress your girlfriend.

The judge coughs. "Miles Derkach, I could revoke your driver's license for a period of ninety days. However, as this is your first offence and there is some suspicion that you were not alone in this caper, I will set a probationary period for that same amount of time. You will report weekly to a probation officer."

My feet itch inside my boots, but his next sentence stops any nervous reaction.

"In addition, you will perform one hundred hours of community work."

What?

"I recommend that you be assigned to work with a senior citizens' organization. Hopefully, the experience will help you gain some respect for people and their property. If this group can't help you, son, no one can. Next case."

I slowly get up and walk out of the courtroom past Mom and Kenny. I'm so relieved to be getting out of there that I fire up a smoke even before I'm out the door. A group of probation officer types give me dirty looks. One breaks away, strides towards me and plants herself solidly in my path. "Miles Derkach, I am Ms. Kirkpatrick, your probation officer. Just where do you think you're going?"

"Out," I say, waving the cigarette.

"Not so fast." She points a sticklike finger at my smoke. "Put that out!"

I turn around and jam the cigarette into an ashtray, even though I've only taken a couple of drags.

"I have your community work assignment ready for you," she snaps. "Come with me."

I glance over at Mom and Kenny and give them the high sign. Mom wipes her eyes and Kenny winks. She's so beautiful! Brown curly hair that just doesn't quit, big brown eyes and on top of all that she's a great mechanic.

I follow *Miz* Kirkpatrick. She takes me

to her office and spreads out some papers. I lean against the doorframe. "Sit!" she commands. I do.

"Miles Derkach, you have one hundred hours of community work to perform and I have the perfect spot for you. The Rossburn Community Association has offered to work with selected teenagers under court supervision."

She hands me a piece of paper. "Here's the president's name and address. Report to him Saturday morning at 9:00 sharp. He will phone me when you arrive, and you will phone me as you leave. You and I will become well acquainted."

Chapter Three

"She's *hot!*" Larry the Lark had whispered when Mackenzie Morash strolled into shop class the second week of school, twenty minutes late, wearing baby-blue coveralls and a wide smile. Normally Mr. Santonio would have sent a student packing if she came in even a minute late. But this time he took the note and paired her with Greg Summers.

Greg groaned. He's a keener, always

wants top marks in everything, and having a girl as his partner was a drag. So he thought. Mackenzie looked over the tools and took that little Briggs and Stratton engine apart in minutes, with all the parts sorted for proper I.D. and reassembly. Greg's grin nearly split his face.

Turns out Mackenzie's dad had just opened his tenth Master's Transmission shop over on Vulcan Avenue. Turns out Mackenzie grew up in garages.

I fell in love with Kenny that first day, but I waited for all the other guys to take their shot.

Maybe it was my good looks and money — ha! — or maybe the fact that I didn't come on strong, but she went for me. I'm pretty comfortable around girls but I'd never gone with anyone before, just the odd date. Until Mackenzie.

One day Larry the Lark and I were leaving school in his '72 New Yorker — it's the size of the *Queen Mary* and just about as old — when we spotted the cheerleaders having a practice. Larry slammed on the brakes. "Sweet!" The girls were finishing up for the day, gathering their pom poms and megaphones. We had a big game coming up on Friday against the hotshot Rutherford Rustlers.

Larry pulled up to the curb. "Any of you fine ladies order limousine service?" Six girls jumped into the backseat, laughing, smelling of perfume and girl sweat and all things nice. Mackenzie was one of them. We drove up and down a few streets, gunning the engine at every green light, stereo blasting tunes, then pulled in to the A&W. I saw Mackenzie looking me over, so I sat back, stayed cool, not yapping like Larry, but sort of listening, keeping Mackenzie in my peripheral vision.

We drove the girls home. Luckily for me, Mackenzie lived the farthest away in a suburb called Green Forest Acres. The transmission business must pay well.

When she opened the car door I hopped out too. "You play on the team, don't you?"

she asked. I nodded. More on the bench, I could have said, but she'd find that out soon enough. "I'll cheer for you extra loud," she said.

Feeling brave I asked, "Are you going to the dance after the game?" When she nodded I said quickly, before losing my nerve, "Could I come by for you?" She took the scrunch thing out of her hair and threw back her head. Her hair bounced and flew around her face. Then she looked at me with those brown eyes. "Sure!" she said.

"Nice work," Larry said when I got back into the car. "You never moved that quick on the field!"

I laughed. "She's cool."

"Naw!" Larry drawled. He threw the car into drive and punched the gas pedal, as always.

Our team won, and I played well enough to not embarrass myself. I could hear Mackenzie's voice cheering me on, even leading a special cheer for me. You know . . . "Give me an M! Give me an I! Give me an L! Give me an E! Give me an S! *Miles Derkach, Miles Derkach . . .*" and the cheering squad went into this locomotive cheer that they do. Felt great.

After the game I went home to clean up.

Mom watched me. "Is this a special night?"

I nodded.

"Got a date?"

Nod again.

"Who with? Anyone I know?"

"Don't think so. They just moved to this area. Mackenzie Morash."

"Oh, the transmission people." Mom smiled.

Of course she'd know the name. She works in the office at RPM Auto Parts.

"I guess you'll need some money, to take her out later for something to eat." She handed me a fifty. She wouldn't take it back.

"This girl might be special, Miles," she said. "Treat her right."

Is she clairvoyant or something?

After court, Mom drives Kenny and me to our house, then goes off to work. We hang out, listen to tunes, play around a bit — but who can concentrate? We talk about court and my sentence. I tell her a bit more about how it happened. But before I blow it and tell her how I'm really innocent, Kenny cuts in.

"That was cool, Miles, admitting your guilt. And you didn't say a thing about anyone else."

So we forget about the court case and the day, and Larry and Spider, and everyone else but Kenny and Miles.

Chapter Four

I wake to the phone clanging like a fire alarm.

"Yeah?" I groan into the receiver.

"Good morning, Miles," says a voice I can't place. "Aren't you supposed to be somewhere by now?"

"Who's this?"

"*This* is Ms. Kirkpatrick, and I'm giving you fifteen minutes to be dressed and standing on your front steps."

"Huh?" My brain burns rubber getting up to speed.

"Just be ready, Miles. I will be pulling into your driveway in exactly fifteen minutes — and I don't like to be kept waiting!"

She hangs up with a slam.

I go over to the fridge, take out the milk and drink it half down right from the carton — a habit that sends Mom to red-line. I notice the lightbulb has burned out in the fridge. I'll change it, later. I throw a couple of whole wheat slices into the toaster. When they're ready, they shoot out like torpedoes. Gotta adjust the spring on that toaster. I'm good at fixing stuff, but I don't have much time.

I shower and throw on a plaid flannel shirt and jeans. My knees show through the holes the way I like 'em. I hear a horn honk. I'm thinking up some words to express how I feel about being hassled when I see Ms. Kirkpatrick peering through the glass in the door. I should sue for invasion of privacy. I grab my jacket and yank open the door. She thrusts something at me.

"Here. Read this newspaper on the way over. Get current."

"What?"

She's thrown me off-track. I trot behind her like a dog, clutching the morning paper, and slide onto the front seat of her car. It takes a moment to realize what I'm sitting in. The rich smell of leather upholstery grabs me first, and I glance at the dash. Since when did social workers start driving Mercedes?

I smile. "Let's race!"

Ms. Kirkpatrick laughs, and the car moves swiftly and silently down the street. I lean my head back and look through the sunroof. I could get used to this! Quad speakers wrap around an old rock tune. I'm tapping my fingers on my bare knee, looking out the window of this great machine, when I see Larry the Lark waiting for the light to change. His eyes shine like Maglites when he spots me. I turn away from the window.

"Where are we going?" I think to ask.

"To your appointment, one hour late!" she states.

"Oh, yeah." I dig into my jacket pocket for the crumpled bit of paper. Rossburn Community Association. Ned Barnier, President.

We pull up in front of a house. The hedge is perfectly trimmed and there are flower beds everywhere. Worse, I spy lawn ornaments: a mother deer with Bambi fawns, Snow White's dwarves holding birdbaths, even a wishing well! I look at the sign on the front door: Ned and Millie Barnier — Welcome, Friends!

I groan and close my eyes.

A man and woman appear at the door. I've seen their type before. Experts at baking banana bread, playing Scrabble and telling old war stories. They'll call me Sonny. I slide down into the leather upholstery.

"Sit up!" Ms. Kirkpatrick snaps. "Say good morning. And smile. Because, Miles, this is your lucky day."

Chapter Five

"Miles, what do you like to do best?" Mr. Barnier pulls up a chair and sits down. I notice that he drags one leg a bit and his speech seems slow.

What *do* I like to do best? Well, how about sleeping in, eating, watching TV, hanging out with Kenny and Lark, fixing old things that other people throw away? I tell him the last one.

"Well, now!" Mr. and Mrs. Barnier flash twin-beam smiles. "Is there anything in particular you like to fix?"

"I'm good at motors," I say. "But I've also fixed appliances, fridges, lawn mowers, even some old radios and TVs."

"What about cars?"

"We worked on an old Ford pickup, a junker, in shop class, got it running pretty good."

"You worked on a Ford truck engine?"

Mr. Barnier's onto something, but I don't know what.

"I'd like you to start your hundred hours of service by doing something rather ordinary," he says slowly. "Would you mind cleaning out my basement? When you finish that, you can start on the garage."

I look over at Ms. Kirkpatrick. I know I have no choice.

"I'll pick you up at 4:00," she says. "After today you can figure out bus schedules and get here on your own." She thanks the Barniers and leaves.

Hour one, only ninety-nine left to go.

Mr. Barnier takes me downstairs, not to a musty basement but an old-fashioned family room. Shining pink and gray square tiles cover the floor. "No carpets — we like to dance!" Mrs. Barnier says brightly. Knotty-pine walls. A U-shaped bar at one end, and an ancient stereo that plays those big long-play records. I laugh out loud, imagining these old fogies waltzing around to Glenn Miller's band. Or whatever they play.

"Here's your job for today, Miles," Mr. Barnier says. "See these boxes? They're full of magazines. I'd like you to sort them by date and by title. They go back to 1953: *Hot Rod, Rod and Custom, Car Craft.*"

He goes upstairs and I kneel down to open the first box. A smell of old paper. Weird old cars. Articles like "Chopping a Deuce Three-Window" and "Open Drive-lines for Your Old Ford" and "12-Volts for Flatheads." I look at the dates, 1953 to 1969, all mixed up. I start a pile for each year, then make piles below that for each different title, but they're mostly *Hot Rod*.

I recognize some of the magazines. Suddenly I'm a little kid again, sitting in the shop watching The Team build stock cars — my dad, or Duke as they called him, and his buddies Crock, Jazzman and Butch. The cars were similar, but the hot rods in these magazines were built for drag racing while Duke's team was into stock cars. But the love of machines and speed was the same.

When Mr. Barnier opens the door and comes down, I smell food. How long have I been here? It seems like just a few minutes.

"Hey, Miles, it's lunchtime. Are you hungry?"

I wipe my dusty hands on my jeans and smile. "Nope, never thought of it!" I say, and I'm being honest. This is the first time in my life I could have skipped lunch and not missed it.

Mr. Barnier kneels down, nearly losing his balance for a moment. He grabs onto a table and slowly settles himself on the floor beside me. "Stroke," he says, smiling a bit crookedly. "Had a stroke a year ago. I'm in pretty good shape now, but I can't do what I used to."

He picks up a magazine. "I remember buying this issue new — seems like just last week. Buzz Lowe and his dad Dean were a hot team."

I look at their pictures — dad and son, both with military haircuts, looking like marines.

Mr. Barnier points to a photo of a car. "Buzz Lowe's roadster pickup went in the 12s, and only 283 cubes. Pretty hot for those times."

"What does that mean, the 12s?"

"That's the elapsed time from a standing start in a quarter mile. Zero to 110 miles per hour in twelve and one-half seconds. This old hot rod would leave your five-liter Mustangs and Z-28s like they were tied to trees."

"I'm impressed," I say.

"I was a hot-rodder all my life," he says. "Built my first rod in 1957 when I was sixteen."

I feel as if Mr. Barnier doesn't know, or care, that I'm in the room. He's talking to himself, or to the memories pictured in the magazines.

" . . . a '39 Ford coupe, full-house flathead, had it real low, loud pipes, painted it black with some amateur pinstriping. That car had no trouble attracting female riders — and the law."

"Was it like these cars in the magazines?"

"You mean you never saw a real hot rod?"

"Oh yeah! I know this guy, his brother has a Trans Am. It's pretty hot." I don't tell him how "hot" it really is and that it belongs to Spider's brother. Spider told me that most of the parts on it were stolen, everything from the stereo to the wheels.

"A *Trans Am!*" Mr. Barnier spits the words. "I'm talking *real* hot rods! The cars that started it all, the roadsters and coupes. The ones that used to race on the dry lakes in southern California. That's where all these street machines came from."

"What kinds of cars?"

"I guess the first hot rods were Model T roadsters with souped-up four-bangers. Then came the flathead Fords, then the overheads." He looks at me. "You like working on engines?"

"Yeah, but I never had a chance to do too much," I say. "At school, in shop, we worked on single-cylinder Briggs and Stratton engines."

"They're for lawn mowers and compressors. You said you worked on a truck engine."

"We found an old V-8 from a '63 Ford truck. We hauled it to the school shop from the junkyard. We got two of them, in fact, and scrounged parts from one to fix the other."

He laughs. "What did you do to the engine?"

"Pulled it apart. It was seized up and we had to free it. We didn't have any money so we had to take parts off the other engine and mix them up to get them to work. I did the heads — the valve job — I ground valves and lapped them in."

"That's a fairly technical operation. What kind of a machine did you use?"

Mrs. Barnier calls down from the top of the stairs. "Come and eat before everything's cold!"

"Okay, Ma!" Mr. Barnier calls. He turns back to let me answer his question.

"We had a Sioux grinder at the school shop. I hand-lapped the seats with compound and a suction cup."

"Well, seeing how you're such an expert on valves — I need to do the heads on my engine. Maybe someday we can ask permission from your teacher and use the school's shop facilities."

"Sure."

"Your dad ever teach you mechanics?"

"Yeah, he did."

Duke Derkach, my father, was a "racing wrench" in the days before racers had big sponsorships. Two or three guys built the car, and the best man drove. Perhaps it wasn't the best place for a kid to hang out, but nearly every weekend Dad would take me to the shop where I'd hand out tools or beers and drink pop and munch potato chips. That's where I got handy fixing things.

Dad and his friends always acted like big-time racers. They called themselves The Team, with Crock as crew chief, Jazzman the engine specialist, Butch the body fabricator, Dad the mechanic and me the mascot whose presence was supposed to bring them good luck.

Mr. Barnier waits in silence as I, like he's just done, lose myself in memories.

"Yeah," I say finally, "my dad taught me a bit about mechanics. He was a stock-car racer."

"What track? I might know him."

"Here, at Speed Boss, but he moved to Toronto and then to the States," I say hurriedly. "I don't know where he's racing now." I stand and offer Mr. Barnier my hand. He takes it to pull himself upright.

"I'm hungry," he says quickly.

"Me too."

We go upstairs and dig into big bowls of homemade soup, a heaping platter of sandwiches and warm peach pie.

Chapter Six

At 4:15, Ms. Kirkpatrick dumps me off at home and I saunter into the house. Mom is home, which is fine, we get along okay most of the time. But today, drinking coffee at our kitchen table, is Mr. Right, also known as Jeff.

Jeff is the head accountant for some oil company. Button-down shirt, color-coordinated tie, $500 suit, pants pressed to cutting edge, shoes shining like mirrors. What does she see in this loser? Probably a backlash against Dad, like one of him was maybe enough. Jeff stands when I enter and extends his hand. I still haven't shaken my nice-guy personality from being at the Barniers' all day so I grab it and smile. Mom raises a surprised eyebrow.

"How did your day go?" she asks. Her tone is guarded like she's pleading with me to say "Fine" and leave it at that.

"Fine," I say and head over to the fridge.

"You don't need to eat. Jeff is taking us out for dinner."

"Sorry, I've got plans." I keep my head in the fridge. I don't want to catch Mom's eyes.

"This is important, Miles," she says. "We have something to discuss that you might find interesting."

"Go ahead."

"Not here."

"Why not here? This is home, ain't it?" I can feel Mom wince. My grammar is usually pretty good. She knows I'm just playing up for Jeff.

Jeff clears his throat. "Miles, how about chicken 'n' ribs at Swiss Chalet?"

"Thanks anyway."

"We can invite Kenny to join us," Mom says.

"She's busy. I'm meeting up with her later."

I go into the living room, pick up the phone and punch the Lark's number.

"Hey, Lar."

"Hey, bro. Was that you in the Mercedes? That hood emblem would make a great belt buckle."

"Yeah, that was me. Thanks to you and that *bug* you hang out with."

"Who? Spider? He's okay when you get to know him. He says you're a real ace guy for taking the rap. Don't worry, he'll make it up to you."

I decide the less I tell Larry about my assignment, the better. He has a way of showing up at the wrong place at the right time. Most of the things the Lark does are wrong, come to think of it, but he's been my closest buddy since grade school. He knows about my dad and all, but he'd never tell my personal business to other people. He just mentioned the stock-car racing bit in front of Spider so I'd look cool.

"So, what's up for tonight?" I ask Larry.

"It's gonna be a good one, man! Megan's having a party."

"Sounds great. Pick me up. Now."

"I'll be right there."

I hang up. Mom follows me down the hall and into my room before I can close the door. "Okay, what's going on?"

"Nothing."

"Tell me about the community service."

"This old couple have got me cleaning out their basement, sorting magazines, that kind of stuff. I'll get through it."

Mom is leaning with her back against my door, blocking any escape. "I had a long talk with Ms. Kirkpatrick and a police officer today. Final conclusion: your behavior is going to improve starting *right now*. That's what we wanted to discuss with you. Jeff has some positive ideas. But since you won't listen to him, you'll listen to me!"

Her voice rises as she builds up steam for the power push. "Whatever it takes — me quitting work to *baby-sit* you twenty-four hours a day, a group worker assigned to monitor you, sending you to an Outward Bound program — I'll do whatever it takes to straighten you out."

She pauses for breath. "The first thing you're going to do is find some new friends. I don't want to see that scamp, Larry Lowisky, around here ever again. You hear? He's nothing but trouble."

I grab my jacket and stuff a pack of smokes into my pocket. Mom doesn't say anything as I walk down the hall. Jeff stands up as if to block my way, then wisely steps aside.

"Your mother wants to talk to you, Miles," he says.

"She just did."

I hear the Lark pulling into the driveway with the old smokin' beast. Perfect timing.

"Hey, Miles, what's happening?"

"Trouble, Larry."

Chapter Seven

The Lark and me are definitely due for a major discussion. Let's see, where should I start? What kind of a friend takes off and leaves you for dead in a stolen car? What kind of buddy gets you involved in stealing a car in the first place? The Mustang owner's insurance company will likely try and nail me for damages. Larry the Lark owes me, big time.

We cruise the drag but nobody's around at this hour. We pull into the A&W.

" . . . so I got these BMW hood ornaments and I try to trade two of them and an Alfa Romeo for one Ferrari, but think Spider will go for it? No way! So I sweeten the deal, offer him a . . . "

His words drift in and out of my head. I'm thinking back to the covers of those dusty old *Hot Rod* mags. One from 1964 shows Don Garlits driving the *Swamp Rat* dragster.

" . . . and so I tell him to put it where the sun don't shine, I'll find some other fence . . . Hey! You're not listenin'!"

"Sorry, Lar." I take a pull on my milk shake. Get brain freeze.

"What are you thinking about? Anything I should know?"

Should I tell? He's interested in cars.

"At this old guy's place where I was today, he had a pile of old hot-rod magazines. I was just thinking about some of those cars."

"Like what?"

"Like 'Big Daddy' Don Garlits breaking two hundred miles per hour in a quarter mile with a dragster called *Swamp Rat* in the early '60s!"

Larry looks doubtful. "And he turned *two hundred in the quarter*, way back then? You sure? What did he use for power?"

"A 392-inch hemi out of a '57 Dodge truck, totally modified."

"What's a 'hemi'?"

"It's a special way Chrysler made heads. I read that they stole the design from Zora Arkus Duntov, the guy responsible for the Corvette. The 'Z' in the Z-28 Camaro comes from Zora."

"Hey!"

"*Swamp Rat* ran on these humungous Racemaster drag slicks. The engine was super charged, fuel injected, with a Crower roller cam."

"What language are you talking, man?"

I laugh. "Mr. Barnier, the dude I'm working for, he's a hot-rodder from way back. He tells me all about these cars. He's a cool old guy."

"He have a rod?"

"I dunno. He wants to do the heads on something that's in his garage. I said I could probably grind the valves for him at the school shop."

"Getting in good with the boss?"

"He's okay. This hundred hours is going to be easy time."

"Find out if he's got a rod," Larry says. "It could have parts worth lifting."

"No."

"No what?" The Lark leans towards me in his seat, staring. I stare back.

"Look, Lar, this last bit, with the Mustang, you and Spider running off and letting me take the rap — I could have gone to the joint!"

"Hey, man, Spider got nabbed on that theft charge two months ago and right now he's on bail. He couldn't stick around! And if I break my probation I'll get time for sure. I knew you'd be okay." Larry pops a fry into his mouth. "And you aren't exactly havin' a rough time over there at that old man's. You said yourself this hundred hours' community work is goin' okay." He leans towards me. "Me and Spider are *grateful*, man."

"I could have lost my driver's license."

"Aw, you got nothing to drive anyway. Come on! Let's forget it — get ripped at Megan's bash, be somebody."

"I don't feel like it."

"C'mon! Don't play dead. Give Kenny a call. It's time we had some fun!"

Larry crunches up the papers and napkins, all that's left of his huge order, and flicks on the headlights for tray pickup.

Sure. I'll call Kenny.

Chapter Eight

Megan is a Space Cadet. She used to do drugs but then she got involved with this club that turned her on to a new world. Now she loves the Space Channel. She'll get up at four in the morning to watch astronauts suit up, walk out and get strapped in for their shuttle launches. Then she yawns all day in school. She says it's good to be focused on something. Her shrink says she has an obsessive personality.

Larry and Megan have been hanging out for almost a year now. Megan has long straight blonde hair, usually with pink, purple or green streaks depending on what galaxy she's in.

The Lark, Megan and I pull up to No. 17 Green Forest Acres. Larry and Megan stay in the car with the motor running because it's hard to start. I sprint up to the door and ring the bell, which chimes something classical.

Mr. Morash answers.

"Come in, Miles. Kenny's nearly ready." He looks out to the smoking '72 New Yorker that's brought me to his door. "Tell your chauffeur to head down to Midas Muffler — he's losing a tailpipe and you'll all be asphyxiated."

"Yes, sir." I grin and he smiles back.

When I first met Kenny's parents I was real nervous — especially after Mr. Morash's first comment.

"Miles Derkach," he said slowly when we were introduced. "I know Duke Derkach from the Speed Boss Racetrack. Any relation?"

"Uh, yeah. He's my dad," I said, expecting to be thrown out of the house. "How did you know him?"

"My father, Aesop Morash Sr., started the family garage business and worked me like a hired hand," Mr. Morash replied. "I wasn't allowed to go racing. How I longed to be at the track with guys like your dad."

"Daddy, Miles doesn't want to hear your life history!" Kenny interrupted, with a cute grin. Her dad smiled back. You could see they were close.

"I do want to hear about it, Mr. Morash," I said.

"Call me Ace," he offered. "All I wanted was to be like the Duke. His team would come into the shop to get sponsorship money. We'd give them parts and some cash for gas and they'd be off again. He lived the life I dreamt of."

Good old Dad. The man in the photo album wearing the double-breasted suit, holding up racing forms and "lucky" tickets, in a picture taken somewhere in the States. The man in the T-shirt and jeans, mechanic's cap on backwards, grease all over his hands and face, holding up a beer.

"I lost track of your father," Ace said, "although I often wondered about him."

"That gives us something in common," I'd replied. Kenny's dad and I have got along pretty well ever since.

He pats my shoulder. "You and Kenny have a nice evening. And get that exhaust system fixed."

"Thanks, Mr. Morash — Ace. I sure will."

We get into the New Yorker. It rumbles like a locomotive and slowly pulls away.

"Yahoo!" Kenny shouts so loudly I jump. "Out of jail for one whole night! Let's party!"

"Some jail," Larry says. "You ain't seen nothin', babe. I'll be in a real jail if I break probation." He shoots a meaningful look my way.

Megan moves over on the big bench front seat to cozy up next to him. "Nobody's going to jail. We're going to party!"

We arrive back at her house to see that several cars have already arrived, including Spider's black Z-28. I want to grab Kenny and get out of there, but I have no wheels. Besides, she's already jumping out of the car to help Megan pack in the groceries. Like Duke used to say, "*The best way through a bad situation is hands on the wheel and best foot floored.*"

Megan's family room is decorated to resemble the space station with posters, souvenirs, signed photos of astronauts, and a large-screen TV flashing videotaped scenes from the space station and Mission Control. She's also taped televised interviews with astronauts who describe how it feels to travel eight kilometers a second and view the earth from space. She's even bought freeze-dried packages of space food for the party. Her favorite thing in the world is a scale-model replica of the Canadarm that Larry made for her from PVC piping. For tonight she insists everyone take on names of astronauts. She, of course, is Julie Payette. Great, but I mean *obsessive*.

Talk gets interesting as we compare hot rods to the space shuttle. "I'd way rather be in a shuttle," Megan says. "Imagine being powered by two seventeen-inch-diameter fuel lines, one for hydrogen and the other for oxygen! Cosmic blast!!"

"I suppose so, compared to a 3/8-inch car fuel line!" Larry says, grinning. "And no road drag."

"Big fuel bill," Greg Summers adds, sounding like the accountant he'll likely become.

Megan's eyes sparkle as she gets into her favorite subject. "A shuttle uses twelve tons of fuel a second," she informs us. "Four and a half million pounds of shuttle and pay-load need lots of help to get off the launch pad."

From the corner of my eye I see Spider standing against the far wall, sipping a beer, looking over the group. He's older than the rest of us and I don't know why he's here. Larry likely invited him, but we're not his usual crowd. His eyes flicker over to me. I stare him down and he looks away.

I'm suddenly furious. When he leaves the room I decide to follow. I trail him upstairs and into the kitchen, which opens onto a deck. He looks back at me, then opens the sliding glass door. Then we're standing outside. He lights a smoke and offers me one. I shake my head. We lean over the deck rail to look at the city lights below. The night is warm, perfect, no insects except for the big one standing beside me.

He speaks first. "Sorry, kid. That whole scene came down bad. You need anything — parts, cash?"

I don't reply. He flicks his butt over the deck rail. For some reason, that act does it.

"Go down there and pick it up." I'm surprised how even my voice sounds.

Spider looks at me. "What?"

"You heard me. There's a deck below, that butt could start a fire."

"It won't — and watch your mouth, you little punk." His eyes narrow and he turns to face me. "You're a slow learner, you know that?"

But Spider's wrong. I'm a quick learner. My right fist lands on his chin. His head snaps back and he grabs the deck rail for balance. I catch him with my left and he's staggering, holding onto the rail to keep from hitting the floor. Then I see his hand snake to his belt and a flash of a silver blade. I nail him hard, square on the temple, sending both him and the knife flying. He hits the boards while the knife skitters over the side of the deck.

Suddenly everyone's outside. Larry and Greg hold Spider back as he lunges at me. "You're dead, kid, know what I mean?" Spider says through a fattening lip.

I wipe my hands on my jeans and turn to Kenny. "Let's get out of here."

In the semi-darkness of the lawn I spot

the glitter of steel. I bend and pick up the knife. It's his switchblade. One quick push on a button in the handle and the blade flies out, thin, sharp, deadly. I hold it in my hand so Kenny can't see, then close and slip it into my jacket pocket.

I take Kenny's hand and we walk across the lawn onto the street. I'll pay for decking Spider, but I still hold a couple of aces. I know who stole the Mustang. I know whose garage likely holds a big stock of hot parts and tools. I don't want to rat, but this is gonna get dirty.

Kenny and I stroll along the sidewalk. As we cross the bridge over Stony Creek I toss the switchblade. I hear it plunk into the dark, fast-running water.

Chapter Nine

Ned Barnier has given me a box of his old magazines. One of my favorite rods is *Lightnin' Bug*, a "T" pickup with the body channeled — lowered six inches over the frame. It's powered by a '52 Cad engine and turned a hundred in the quarter mile. Pretty hot for 1954! This car was in almost all the scenes of *77 Sunset Strip,* an old television show starring Kookie Burns.

I want to build one of these old-style rods!

I've been working for Ned for two hours a night after school and six hours on Saturday. He lines up all sorts of work for me — landscaping around the community hall, painting interior walls, and yesterday he had me check and oil the bearings on their furnace. He's impressed with how quickly I figure things out.

"When I had my stroke, they took my license," he tells me, "but I'm in therapy. I'll get it back soon."

"Maybe you'll make a rod run this summer yet," Mrs. B adds.

"A rod run?" My ears perk up.

Mrs. B smiles. "Ned, I think it's time."

He pauses for a moment. "All right. After lunch we'll take the wraps off the coupe."

It's the coolest machine I've ever seen. All I can do is stare. The bright red paint and the body lines are beautiful. It sits just right.

He opens the driver's door and I look inside. The upholstery is red and white pleated leather. The dash is full of high-end gauges and a Sun Super tachometer. My mind flashes back to Larry's comment about there being lots of good racing parts. I feel a pain in my gut and decide that the Lark will know nothing about this car.

Millie goes over to the garage wall and takes down a sign covered in plastic. "These are the specs of the car, Miles. We put this sign up beside it at car shows."

I scan the list: "1937 Ford coupe, '58 Corvette 283-cubic-inch engine, 270 horse-power." I turn to look at Ned and grin. "Dual quad carbs, Borg-Warner T-10 four-speed, Hurst synchro-loc shifter." This is a *thoroughbred.*" '57 Olds rear end, 3.70 to 1 ratio; '56 Ford F-100 front brakes, steering column and steering box."

"The front axle is dropped four inches for a nice rake," Ned explains.

It sits butt in the air like a greyhound at the starting line.

"Does it run?" I ask.

"I haven't run it for over a year. I want to pull the heads and freshen them up first. That's what I was talking to you about. Maybe you and I could do it together."

"Sure," I say.

"I'll pay you by the hour, myself," Ned says. "Your community work is for the association. But this will be our project. You with me?"

"How fast will it do a quarter mile?" I ask.

"It'd probably do something around thirteen seconds," Ned explains, "although this is a street machine, not a racer."

"I'd love to own a rod," I say, "but I don't have the money."

"It doesn't take much money to get started, but it takes some scrounging," Ned says. "I could help you scout around for a car. Do it like in the old days, build it while you drive it. You could even leave it stock, just lower it a bit and give it some cool paint. Later build an engine as a school shop project.

You could do some of the work here."

I see a vision of me starring in an update of *American Graffiti*.

"Let's pull those heads!" I say.

I can't remember the last time I felt this happy, except for the time I spend with Kenny.

When I get home I'm going to replace the fridge bulb and fix our toaster.

Chapter Ten

Sunday brunch. Mom and Jeff still haven't got around to telling me their big news.

We eat mainly in silence. After dessert I slide back my chair. "Excuse me."

"Where are you going?" Mom asks.

"Out." I head towards the door.

I hear Jeff's footsteps so I hurry down the front steps. "Miles, for your mother's sake . . ." He stands, hands on hips.

Mom comes to stand beside him at the door.

"Hey, Mom, I don't need a new dad."

Then I'm down the driveway, running. I don't stop until I'm at the Dairy Queen three blocks away. I phone Larry, still panting.

"What's up?"

"Hey, bro. Where ya been?"

"Can you come and get me?"

"Yeah, sure. Where are you?"

I tell him and go inside to order a Blizzard.

The Lark pulls into the parking lot. I hear his tires chirp on the pavement as he brakes in front. The waitresses and customers all stare as Larry flings open the door of the restaurant and enters, grinning. He nods to the customers as if he's a visiting rock star or something and slides into my booth. "Hey, you look down, man! You lose your job or something? That old dude fire you?"

"Naw, I'm just sick from watching Mom with her new boyfriend."

"Wanna scare him? We could do a little number on his car."

"No! Aw, he's okay I guess. I just don't like to see some guy making Mom happy." That sounds dumb. "Let's get out of here," I say. We spin out of the parking lot, laying rubber.

It's a great day so we drive out to Fastback Beach. The place is named for the high sand ridges covered with clumps of dry grass that ripple from the hills down towards the beach. All our friends come here, while families go to Main Beach to pad around and build their sand castles. But today Fastback doesn't have much appeal. Too many bad memories of my last trip here.

"Nothing doing here today," Larry says in a downer voice. "No one around."

It's been like that a lot lately. I don't know what's happening. Fewer parties, fewer kids hanging out. Most have after-school jobs and are saving money for college.

"What're you doing this summer?" Larry asks.

"I guess I'll do some work for Ned."

"Aren't your hundred hours almost up?"

"Yeah, but he's asked me to do some stuff on his car. He'll pay me."

"What kinda car?"

And suddenly I'm telling Larry about the coupe. I'm partway through describing it before I remember I wasn't going to say a word about the rod to anyone. Larry looks real interested, though, so I go on to describe all the cool engine parts. "Ned wants to re-do the heads and get the rod ready for the Show and Shine," I say.

I finally wind down. Larry throws his cigarette butt out the window. He hasn't said a word.

"What are *you* doing this summer?" I finally ask.

Larry gives me a foxy look. "I'm going to be attending a few Show and Shines," he says evenly. "You can tell me all about the rods, who the owners are, where they live. Then at night you can come with me to scout garages. Should be able to bag some whizzy parts. Thanks, pal. You've just given me my summer job."

My breath catches. I glare at him, hard. "Anyone tries to lift parts off Ned's car or from the other hot rods and I'll turn them in."

Larry's eyes burn. "Get out!"

I have lots of time to think as I walk back to the highway and stick out my thumb for a ride to town.

Chapter Eleven

On Saturday morning I show up at the Barniers', on time, to find Ms. Kirkpatrick sitting in their kitchen.

"Hello, Miles," she says. She smiles and holds out some papers. "Today is the first day of the rest of your life."

Huh?

"Your hundred hours are up! And you've done very well. Mr. and Mrs. Barnier give you all As for your performance."

"You were marking my performance?" I look from one to the other.

Ned laughs. "Not on paper."

I sit at the table wondering what will come next. Suddenly I recall something odd — I didn't see the Mercedes outside.

"Where's your car?" I ask.

A sad look comes over her face. "It was stolen yesterday from the parking lot at the mall," she says. "And the thing is, it wasn't just an ordinary car. It was my father's. He left it to me when he died last year."

I sit frozen, even though my hands are clutched tightly around the hot coffee cup. *That emblem would make a great belt buckle*, I hear the Lark say.

"Do the police have any idea where it might have gone?" Ned asks.

"They said it's likely in a big container being shipped to Russia or Central America." Her voice chokes.

Voices sound in my ears . . . *good belt buckle . . . got a Slim-Jim . . . let's go!*

Ms. Kirkpatrick blows her nose, snuffles a bit and takes a sip of coffee. "The police said that my job makes me a good target for something like this. I deal daily with people who . . . well, who know the ropes, the who and how of thievery."

"And their friends sometimes aren't so quick to learn right from wrong," Ned interjects.

I know my face must be burning. I can barely see the coffee cup in my hand. My eyes blur with the heat from my face, my ears ring and I can feel my blood racing, hear my heart pounding, and of course my feet are itching like crazy. I've got to get out of here.

I hear Dad giving me his version of fatherly advice. *On the short track it's every man for himself. You've got to understand the whole picture.* And Spider's words: *You're dead, kid, know what I mean? A slow learner.*

"Yes, sometimes friends aren't so quick to learn." Ms. Kirkpatrick interrupts the whirl of words zinging through my head. I feel like she is looking knowingly at me.

"Are you feeling ill?" Mrs. Barnier asks me, care showing on her face.

"Yeah," I say.

"Can we give you a ride home?"

"Sure. I'll make up my last few hours tomorrow or next week, whenever."

"No problem."

Ms. Kirkpatrick gets up to leave. "I'm driving a department vehicle," she says. "No passengers."

Fine with me.

I get into the backseat of the Olds and rest my head on the knitted seat covers. Mr. and Mrs. B take forever to get in and belted up. On the way home I close my eyes. I don't want to see the Lark or anybody.

We arrive at my house. I get out, thank them and go around to the back so they won't see me using my key, realize no one's home and feel they should stay with me. I want to be alone to think this through.

The house is cool and quiet. I go straight to the couch and flop.

When I wake up it's noon.

I go to the fridge, drink a half liter of juice and sit down at the kitchen table with the carton still in my hand. I need Kenny.

Chapter Twelve

Sunday morning I show up at the Barniers',
on time. After inquiring about my health, Mr.
Barnier smiles. "A surprise today, Miles. After today your hours of community service will
be completed. We'll be on our own time."

I follow him out to the garage where he
unrolls the cover from the rod, like a sculptor
unveiling his masterpiece. The paint glows.

Ned lifts the hood. His sudden yell

makes me jump. He points, gasping. A mouse has made a nest on the intake manifold!

It takes a moment for Ned to regain his voice. I smother a laugh.

He turns and gives me my first order as his hot-rod mechanic. "Get that thing out of there!"

I do and we proceed.

"Okay, Miles, the first thing to remember is *Primum non nocere*. That's Latin. It means *First, do no harm*. Always keep that in mind when you're working on a rod. We'll remove the hood and lay these mats over the fenders so we don't scratch the paint. That's a $1,500 paint job!"

"Where do we start?"

"Our job today is simple. First, grab a pan and we'll drain the coolant." I follow his orders. "Stick that drain pan underneath the rad and open the petcock. Undo the cap so it drains quicker. Disconnect the upper hose."

Ned explains the engine parts, the modifications he made and the shape it's in after sitting a year, since his stroke.

I get totally involved. It's a privilege to work with so many handcrafted parts made just for this engine. I pull the machine screws and remove the valve covers. Then we take out the distributor.

"We'll pull the manifold with the carbs on," Ned says. "Just disconnect the lines and linkage. This engine has less than 20,000 miles on it, but I think it has a leaking valve."

"How would that happen?"

"Today's gas has no lead in it. The cast-iron valve seats won't survive the unleaded gas."

"How do we fix that?"

"The best fix is to install Stellite seats they use in the propane conversions. They're expensive, but they'll last forever."

Next we drop the headers. We undo the bolts and they lay back.

"Now we'll remove the cylinder heads. You can do that. It's a little heavy for me."

Before I know it, Mrs. Barnier is calling us in to lunch. We clean our hands and head into the kitchen.

"The Show and Shine is in two weeks," Ned says. "The club expects to see about fifty cars there. It's going to be in the parking lot of the Mallory Mall. The crowds love these cars. You'll see a few thousand people turn up."

"Do they ever do damage to the cars, like twist off an aerial or scratch the paint?"

"We haven't had any of that kind of trouble. I think people really respect these old cars and try to be careful, but we keep a close eye on our vehicles."

I'm on the crew! Just like being on the Duke's Team.

"My dad's car was a Chevy Nova," I inform Ned. "The Team modified it into a hot racing stock car. It was painted bright purple with yellow lettering. It was called *The Purple People Eater,* after a song."

"Miles, I know you're going to become a real hot-rodder," Ned says. "Poor lad. It will keep you broke, and working day and night, your whole life!" But he smiles when he says it.

By midafternoon the heads are off. We've got two weeks to get the car running.

"I'm sure the guides are good," he says. "We'll have to replace the seals and we'll check the push-rods and rockers. Did you talk to your shop teacher about grinding the valves?"

"Sure did. No problem as long as I work on them after school under his supervision."

As we pull the valves Ned asks, "Any plans for this summer?"

"I'm hoping to score a job of some kind. My girlfriend, Kenny — Mackenzie Morash — has a job waitressing at Pelican Beach Resort at the lake. Maybe I can work at the marina keeping the rental boats running."

"Your girlfriend is Ace Morash's daughter?"

"Yeah. You know him?"

Ned laughs. "Since he was a hot-rod kid — but he's a solid businessman now."

"Yeah, and still a good guy."

Ned laughs. "What do you plan on doing when you graduate next year, Miles?"

"I'm not sure," I reply. "But I hope that fast cars are in my future, same as in my past."

I can still hear the roar of the crowds, cheering The Team to the finish line. The checkered flag waved. The Team had won. Our pit was suddenly overflowing with people. Everyone wanted to get The Team's autographs and pictures.

"Here's the real hero," Duke said, holding me by the shoulders in front of him as flashbulbs popped. "Miles, my son, our mascot, he brings us good luck." A blonde-haired lady leaned down and gave me a peck on the cheek. "For continued good luck," she said.

My picture was in the paper next day, standing with Dad's hands on my shoulders. The blonde lady was kissing me, and another beautiful lady was kissing Dad. Mom opened the front page of the Sports section . . . and Dad left a week later.

Chapter Thirteen

"Hey, man, let's go!" Larry calls from his car.

Kenny and I are sitting on the curb in front of the school, waiting for Ned.

"Can't tonight, Lark."

"It's your call, man."

Larry's car has an automatic transmission and his big trick is to apply the brake and gas at the same time. This makes the engine roar and the car kind of twists up. I hear some kids laugh as they watch, half-hanging out classroom windows.

Megan grabs my arm as she rushes past. "Come on! There's room for you and Kenny in the back!" She attempts to pull us along.

"Sorry, we've got some work to do in the shop."

Four others in the car groan and jeer. "Trying to make the honor roll?"

"No, we've got some extra mechanical work to do," Kenny says.

"Yeah? What?"

"We have to grind some heads," she says before I can stop her.

Larry tells his passengers to shut up and leans out the window with a sudden look of interest on his face. "You're doing the heads for the *rod?* Catch you later then." Larry blasts off.

When Ned arrives I introduce him to Kenny.

Ned shakes her hand. "Hello, I'm Ned Barnier."

"Hi. My dad has talked about you."

"He has?" Ned looks pleased.

Kenny nods. "Sure. You're one of the original hot-rodders around here."

"Are you like your grandfather — born with a wrench in your hand?"

Kenny grins.

We go back to the shop to meet our instructor, Mr. Santonio.

"Well, Ned Barnier! It's a privilege," Mr. Santonio says.

"You know each other?" I ask.

"Everyone on the hot-rod scene knows Ned Barnier. We watched him run at the Shepard drag strip in the '60s. And I've seen that little '37 coupe of Ned's at events."

We get to work.

"While we have these heads apart let's measure valve-stem clearance," Ned says to his two eager students.

We use a micrometer to check the valve-stem wear on every valve by measuring a worn and unworn section.

"One-thousandth wear is okay, "Mr. Santonio says. "Two thou' is borderline."

They're fine. Now we set each head up on a machine to mill out the seats.

We become so involved that nobody notices the shop door open. Suddenly Larry's head is joining ours over the bench. Mr. Santonio glances up at him. "Hmm, the cat came back. Thinking of registering for classes again, Larry?"

Larry grins. "You never know. This kind of stuff might inspire me."

He watches as I carefully cut out the valve seats.

"Good work," Ned says.

I feel like a surgeon.

Mr. Santonio introduces Larry to Ned. Larry almost falls over himself saying how honored he is to meet him. Ned appears wary.

"Larry, you want to see the new Stellite seats?" Mr. Santonio asks quickly. "They're going to fit right into the holes that Miles is cutting. Hard to believe these cost $150."

"Gee, a little box of metal rings costs that much? That motor must be worth a few grand!"

"Yeah, you can easily spend $3,000 or $4,000 on an engine."

I don't like the glint in Larry's eyes.

Our next job will be to press in the new valve seats, but we've done enough for tonight. We make arrangements for the next session.

"Wow," Larry says as we leave the school. "Cool engine. Bet it'll really wail!" Larry climbs into the New Yorker and peels out.

Kenny and I walk to my place.

Mom really likes Kenny, and I'm glad. Mom and I have been depending on each other for a long time, six years to be exact, from the day Duke pulled out.

Winning that stock-car race was the beginning of The Team going professional, and the end of my family. We trailered the car back to the shop and by then I'd had enough. I'd been in the sun all day and was burnt and tired and hungry, but The Team had to celebrate. Carloads of people arrived with lots of noise and booze. There were bags of chips and I drank some pop intended for mixed drinks — but it was no place for a kid.

About 9:00 that night I was asleep on an old car seat at the side of the shop, a coat thrown over me for a blanket, when Mom's voice woke me. She'd come to get me and found Dad and his friends all partying.

"Don't let me spoil your party, Mr. Big Time, but our son has to go to school in the morning."

I got up and stumbled across the shop floor. When we got home I showered and fell into bed, but awoke at dawn to screaming. I was ten years old, tough and didn't cry much, but I knew my dad was leaving and I lost it. I soaked the pillow.

Duke tried to explain when he left that it would only be for a little while, until he and Mom sorted things out. I stood there noticing his black boots were shined up and his suitcase packed and ready to go. He reached out and shook my hand.

"So long, kid. See you soon."

I had nothing to say.

I tell Kenny all about this. She's cool, encouraging me by listening. I finally run out of words.

Kenny lays her head on my shoulder. "I love you, Miles."

I stroke her hair and we stay that way for a while. Then she says, "What about you and Larry? How did you and Larry get to be friends?"

"Larry has been my friend since first grade," I say.

Larry was a fun kid in school. The Lark, we called him. He'd whistle and hum songs, and the teachers were always telling him to be quiet, but he couldn't quit. It was a riot.

He and I shared lots of stuff including the fact that his home was breaking up too. But it was Larry's mom who left with his little sister, and he just had his dad. We sometimes joked about our two left-behind parents getting together, but we both knew that wouldn't work. Larry's dad was laid off from the chemical plant more than he was employed, but he was a union member and wouldn't take anything else, so things weren't too rich over there. That's when Larry went looking for some action.

The first time Larry stole something and "fenced it," he shared the news with me.

"Miles, it's easy! Spider lives across the alley and he showed me how. Car parts, that's the best gig. Can't be traced and people always want them."

"Car parts? From where?"

"Stores. Parts places. Cars parked on the street. He's even getting a tow truck so he can haul away any car that he wants. Nobody stops a tow truck! Spider knows. So I get the things Spider lists and he pays me cash."

"He probably pockets most of it."

"So?" Larry's eyes narrowed. "He has the *important* job. He's the one who'll get in trouble if he sells parts to an undercover cop or something. He's the one who takes the risk."

Man, I thought to myself, does Spider ever have the Lark in his web.

Larry stopped singing when he started hanging around with Spider. He became secretive and distrustful. His marks dropped and he quit school. The Spider won.

The Lark doesn't show up at the shop the next night, a bad omen.

"Larry seemed to be quite interested," Mr. Santonio says. "You know, that boy showed real talent for bodywork and paint. He turned in some nice class projects before he dropped out."

Over the next few nights we install the seats, grind them and then Kenny and I share the work of fine-grinding to fit the valves into the seats. She has definitely inherited Ace's skills, and Ned admires the care and attention we give to this exacting work.

It's great working with Ned. He never loses his patience, and he takes the time to explain details. He gives me books on rebuilding small-block Chevy engines and tells us about older engines he's worked on. I'm surprised a person can remember that long ago and I say so.

"The 1950s and '60s were wild times for cars," he says. "Then interest in hot-rodding seemed to fade away a bit in our group. We had to concentrate on practical things like mortgages and families." He laughs. "But when we got our 'homework' done, the old dreams came alive again."

Great for me. And Kenny.

Chapter Fourteen

On the morning of the Show and Shine I'm wide awake.

Mom starts the coffeemaker while I toast Pop-Tarts. The toaster works perfectly.

"We've worked our butts off to get the car running and looking great," I tell Mom. "Wait 'til you see it! Ned's got his license back and he's picking me up in the rod!"

"That's nice. Miles, I think Jeff should

enter his car in the Show and Shine. He has a nice new Volvo and he waxes it every weekend."

"I know."

"What's wrong with that? He loves his car, too."

"Mom, if you or Jeff don't know the difference between a cool red '37 Ford hot rod and a brown Volvo . . ." I hear a car outside. "Ned's here!"

I race out the door and Mom follows. But instead of Ned in the driver's seat of his red Ford, he's in the back of a police car.

What's going on?

Mom and I stand on the porch, speechless and staring, as two policemen get out of the car. Ned stays inside.

"Miles Derkach?"

"Yeah," I answer cautiously.

"We would like to ask you some questions about the theft of a vehicle last night or early this morning. Can we come inside?"

Mom steps up. "I'm Miles's mother. He was home all evening!"

I can barely speak past the lump in my throat. "What car?"

"Mr. Barnier's 1937 Ford coupe," the policeman says.

I lose it. I run to the police car. My suddenly blurred vision makes it hard to find the door handle, but I do and yank open the door. "Ned! This can't be happening!"

Ned won't meet my eyes. "It's gone, Miles."

We go inside and Mom makes coffee while we learn what happened. Ned heard some noises late last night, but his medication makes him groggy and he didn't get up to investigate. When he went out to the garage at 7:00 this morning the hot rod was gone.

"And you think Miles had something to do with it?" Mom asks softly, looking at Ned.

"I don't want to believe it, Mrs. Derkach," Ned says. "It's just that the people he's friends with . . . I thought he might be involved or know something."

"I swear I don't know anything about

it." I'm shaking all over, making what I just said sound pretty feeble.

"Have you any ideas who we might contact?" the policeman says.

Larry the Lark. He's got to be involved. I know he's jealous of the time I've spent working on the rod.

"I don't," I say. "But I swear I'll find that car."

"If you're involved you will have violated your probation. A *very* serious matter." The officer lets that sink in. Then he adds, "We'll be contacting your probation officer, Ms. Kirkpatrick, whose car was *also* stolen recently. Interesting coincidence."

"What's going to happen?" Mom is near tears.

"First we'll take Miles to the station for a written statement. Then we'll put an APB out for the missing vehicle. It shouldn't be hard to spot!" the cop replies. And that's it.

We leave the house. Ned and I get in the backseat but don't look at each other. I've never felt so terrible.

At the station I compose the best essay I've ever written. I explain how we worked on the car, how important it was to both of us. I write down everything except my last conversation with Larry. I don't mention any friends at all.

But that doesn't stop me from thinking about them. It doesn't stop the pictures that form in my mind of the car being stripped and sold for parts. They'd get a lot of money for the racing gear, the Stewart-Warner gauges, Hurst shifter, Sun Super tach and the wheels and tires.

Then I form a different mind picture: they're all partying at the beach, taking turns at the wheel, throwing up rooster-tails of sand as they dump the clutch and race the engine until it screams. I see them jumping Fastback's dunes, cutting donuts on the beach, weaving in and out of sand and water.

I sign my statement and hand it to the cop. He looks at it, shrugs and tosses it onto his desk. Just like a teacher, he can tell at a glance when a paper really says nothing.

"We're not charging you, Miles, but you are a suspect. You understand?"

I nod.

"Okay, let's go. We're taking you home."

Again Ned and I get into the backseat of the cruiser. We say nothing until the car stops at Ned's house.

"Miles, your friends are not your friends if they did this," Ned says to me.

I look away out my side window. "I know."

He doesn't need to say any more. Pictures of the low-slung coupe bouncing and scraping over grass-tufted dunes move through my mind like a horror video in slow motion.

Chapter Fifteen

Mom and Jeff are at the door when the cops bring me home. I fight an urge to turn and run. I've got an idea.

First I apologize to Mom for bringing on this trouble and then I try to convince her of my plan. "I want to go out to Fastback Beach," I say. "I know I'll find someone or something there. Can I please have the Honda? I'll be careful."

It works.

As Mom goes to find her keys I hear a car drive up. I look out. It's a brand-new Caddy. Kenny jumps out. I hear her say, "Thanks, Mom," and she comes running up the steps. I don't need to fill her in. Mrs. Barnier already has.

I tell her what I'm going to do. "I'm coming," she says.

On the way out, my foot wants to stomp the gas pedal but I don't need any more attention from cops.

It's a cool day with a wind. As we come off the highway and over the crest of the hill we see a bonfire blazing on the beach. A group of people stand around, all turned the same way watching something. We follow their gaze to a red '37 Ford coupe squirreling at top speed over the dunes, cutting hairpin turns. Sand spews sky-high. The powerful engine screams and gears thrash as the four-speed is jammed through its paces.

We race past the bonfire, past the group of kids who stare at us open-mouthed. I recognize Megan and Greg and some others before they blur into background.

The coupe is flying straight towards us. The car flies over the dune above us. He doesn't see us! I hit the brakes and swerve so suddenly that Kenny nearly pitches through the windshield. She's out of the car almost before it stops, racing towards the coupe.

I cut the ignition and jump out. "Kenny! Watch out!"

I lunge towards her, making the best football tackle of my life. We both roll in the sand as the coupe whizzes past. The engine screams, then we hear a sickening thud.

Everything goes quiet. I hear a seagull's cry and pounding feet of the kids racing from the bonfire towards us. Kenny is lying face-down in the sand. I gently turn her over and brush hair back from her face. "You okay?"

"Yeah, I think so."

I hold her in my arms as we sit, sand-covered and shaking.

"You guys hurt?" Megan and Greg

stoop to check us out and offer their hands to help us to our feet.

Larry and Spider jump out of the coupe and come running over. Suddenly the air is filled with yells and accusations. Larry gives me a push on the shoulder that sends me reeling. "You idiot! If she's hurt it's your fault!"

My fist lands squarely on his nose. A shadow hurls itself at me and I go down under the full impact of Spider's two-hundred-pound frame. We hit the ground.

"You ratted us out!" Spider yells.

Spider outweighs me by fifty pounds — but I'm a hundred pounds madder than him.

Arms pull us apart. Megan is dabbing at a bruise on Kenny's forehead with a wet cloth — actually her bikini top.

Larry wipes at his bloody nose and shoots me an evil look. "You didn't need to get so torqued," he says. "We were just seeing what that engine could do. Not hurtin' anything."

"Why'd you do it, Larry?"

"I just told Spider you were workin' on an old car, that's all. He wanted to see it."

I look down. Larry is wearing a Mercedes belt buckle. "The Mercedes, too," I say.

"Forget it. That thing's toast. Gone, big box." He snorts, coughs.

Spider's sprawled on his stomach on the sand. Greg Summers is sitting on him, holding back his arms in a half nelson. Maybe he's not destined to be an accountant after all.

"Turn him over," I say. "He's likely packing a blade."

Two other guys search him and take away a small knife hidden in a leather sheath under his belt. Talk about somebody being a slow learner.

Spider starts to say something when we hear the car horn. Police!

But it's not a police car. It's Mom, driving Mr. and Mrs. Barnier in their Olds.

Ned gets out of the Olds and strides over

to the coupe. He circles his beloved hot rod, touching it gently here and there like a doctor. I can see scratches and scrapes along the body, and the right front fender and bumper have a few small dents. Ned gets down on the ground to take a look underneath the car. "Muffler torn off," he grunts. "Header pipe's bent. Likely the oil pan's dented up but it's not leaking."

He gets up and wipes the sand from his hands. I help him open the hood. The motor appears to have survived. He reaches inside the car and starts the engine. "Gauges all right." Ned leans over the fender to watch and listen to the engine run.

I give Ned a hand as he gets into the car to drive it ahead so the right front wheel is up on a sand ridge. Then he slides underneath to check things over. Damage seems minimal, to the car that is. It's going to be a while before he can trust me again.

I kneel down. "Mr. Barnier, it's my fault."

He glares up at me.

"I'm not a car thief, Ned. I never was. I had nothing to do with stealing your car or Ms. Kirkpatrick's or even the Mustang — but in a way I did. By knowing Larry and Spider, and maybe by talking too much."

"You sure brought a couple of snakes into my garden," he grunts.

"I did and I'm sorry. I think Larry had something to do with Ms. Kirkpatrick's car — check his belt buckle."

Ned stares up at me. "Are you going to rat?"

I look down at him, lying there in the sand beneath his wrecked hot rod. "I'm gonna rat."

Chapter Sixteen

The police, called by Mom on her cell phone, are not happy to see us. After talking with Ned they make out an accident report. Then they handcuff Larry and Spider and throw them into the back of the police car.

I walk over to Larry's side and look through the window. He glances up at me, then down at his hands.

"I'm sorry, bro," Larry says quietly.

I nod. "You should be."

Megan comes over, looking furious with him and with the entire scene. "This whole place is scary! I'm splittin' — on the next shuttle to Mars!"

"Good idea."

She glares at Larry, turns and jumps into someone's car for a ride back to town. So much for love.

"It's a beautiful old car," Larry says, glancing towards the coupe. "When I was driving it I felt like a million bucks."

"Yeah."

Larry looks like he's lost his last friend. Maybe he has. "I'll help fix it, if the old man will let me. I'll have nothin' else to do after I get out."

"Sure."

Our eyes lock for a moment. Things might work out between us — someday.

"Well, so long," I say.

"So long, bro."

Kenny and I join the gang clustered around the coupe. Ned hands me the keys. "I want you to drive it home, Miles. Could Kenny drive your car back? Mrs. Barnier and your mother could ride in the Olds?"

"Of course," Kenny says, smiling.

Ned and I get into the '37. I light the engine and ease the Hurst shifter into first. The Corvette engine sounds strong. There'll be good times down the road.

Ned tunes in to the oldies station. Jerry Lee Lewis's voice and piano fill the coupe — *Whole lotta shakin' goin' on . . .*

We pull onto the highway. We're cruisin'!

orca soundings

Orca Soundings is a teen fiction series that features realistic teenage characters in stories that focus on contemporary situations.

Soundings are short, thematic novels ideal for class or independent reading. Written by such stalwart authors as William Bell, Beth Goobie, Sheree Fitch and Kristin Butcher, there will be between eight and ten new titles a year.

For more information and reading copies, please call Orca Book Publishers at 1-800-210-5277.

Other titles in the Orca
Soundings series:

Other books by Shirlee Smith Matheson

Nonfiction:
Youngblood of the Peace
This Was Our Valley
Flying the Frontiers Vol. I, "A Half Million Hours of Aviation Adventure"
Flying the Frontiers Vol. II, "More Hours of Aviation Adventure"
Flying the Frontiers Vol. III, "Aviation Adventures Around the World"
A Western Welcome to the World: A History of Calgary International Airport

Juvenile/Young Adult Fiction:
Prairie Pictures
City Pictures
Flying Ghosts
The Gambler's Daughter
Keeper of the Mountains

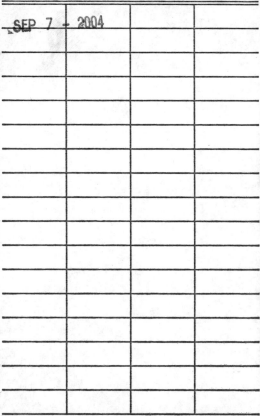

DATE DUE

SEP 7 - 2004			